This **Chicken House** book
belongs to

For the Pearces, Gavin and Thwiggy ~ C.P

For my niece Sophie - who also likes
to stay up all night ~ R.E

© 2011 The Chicken House

First published in the United Kingdom in 2011 by
The Chicken House, 2 Palmer Street, Frome, Somerset, BA11
www.doublecluck.com

Text © 2011 Clemency Pearce
Illustrations © 2011 Rebecca Elliott

Designed by Verity Clark

Printed in Singapore by Imago

1 3 5 7 9 10 8 6 4 2

British Library Cataloguing in Publication Data available
Library of Congress Cataloguing in Publication data available

HB ISBN 978-1-906427-70-2
PB ISBN 978-1-906427-71-9

Fragoline was **bright** and **clean**,
She **always** ate up **all** her **greens**.
Pure as **milk** and **good** as **gold**,
She **always** did as she was told.

But . . .

In the darkest bones of night,
When the world was sleeping tight,
She donned her jet-black velvet cape
And made a midnight-hour escape!

The moon gazed down in fear and dread,
Warning, 'Little ones should be in bed!'
'I'll do exactly as I please!
I'm Fragoline!' she said.

Down the
twisted oak
she scooted,
Past the
scowling
owls that
hooooted,

Swinging swiftly through the air
A little minx with bright red hair.

She tore around upon the grass
Blowing raspberries as she passed.

The moon gazed down in fear and dread,
Warning, 'Little ones should be in bed!'
'You can't tell me what to do!
I'm Fragoline!' she said.

On the forest floor her feet
Stamped a **tip-tap SNAPPY** beat,

That woke fierce creatures from their sleep,
To howl and growl and prowl and **leap** . . .

She let out such an awful sound,
The beasts went yelping back to ground!

Arrrgh!

The moon gazed down in fear and dread,
Warning, 'Little ones should be in bed!'

'I'm not scared of anyone!
I'm Fragoline!' she said.

Through the creepy, sleepy wood,
She skipped to where the churchyard stood.

On the tombstones, row on row,
She danced and pranced
her naughty show.

Resting in their earthy beds,
The ghouls felt footsteps on their heads.

The moon gazed down with fear and dread,
Warning, 'Little one, you'll wake the dead!'

'I don't care about those ghosts!
I'm Fragoline!' she said.

From their dusty graves they rose,
And chased her, wailing, to and fro.
These moaning, groaning bony people
Chased Fragoline right up the steeple.

With
nowhere
left on Earth
to hide,
Poor
Fragoline
was
petrified!

The girl gazed round with fear and dread,
She cried, 'I think it's time for bed!'
Then leapt across the starry sky . . .

and landed safe upon Moon's head.

'Fragoline, you wicked pest!
You've had your fun, now have a rest!'

'I'm sorry I was such a loon!
Sorry creatures!
Sorry Moon!'

The little minx with hair so red
At last was snug and warm in bed.
To help her drift off safe and sound,
All her friends now gathered round.

'Now promise us that you'll be good,
And always do just as you should.'

Fragoline said, 'I just might . . .

At least until
tomorrow night!'

for Oscar and Sara

MEG and the DRAGON

Jan Pieńkowski
and David Walser

PUFFIN BOOKS

It was almost Halloween

Meg
didn't see
Mog's
tail

Cuckoo

MEEEOW

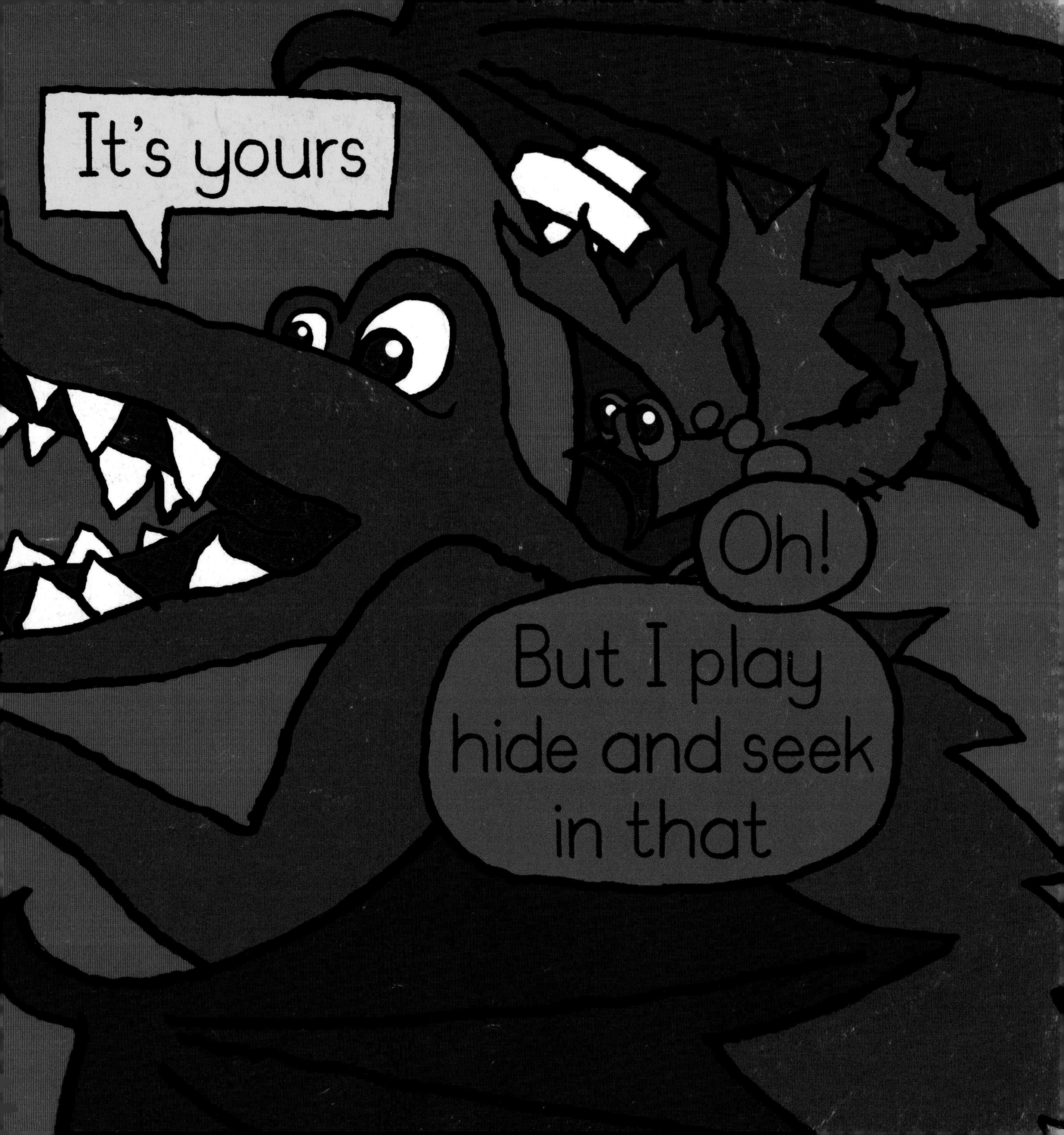
It's yours
Oh!
But I play hide and seek in that

Go! Go!

And Ping learnt how to

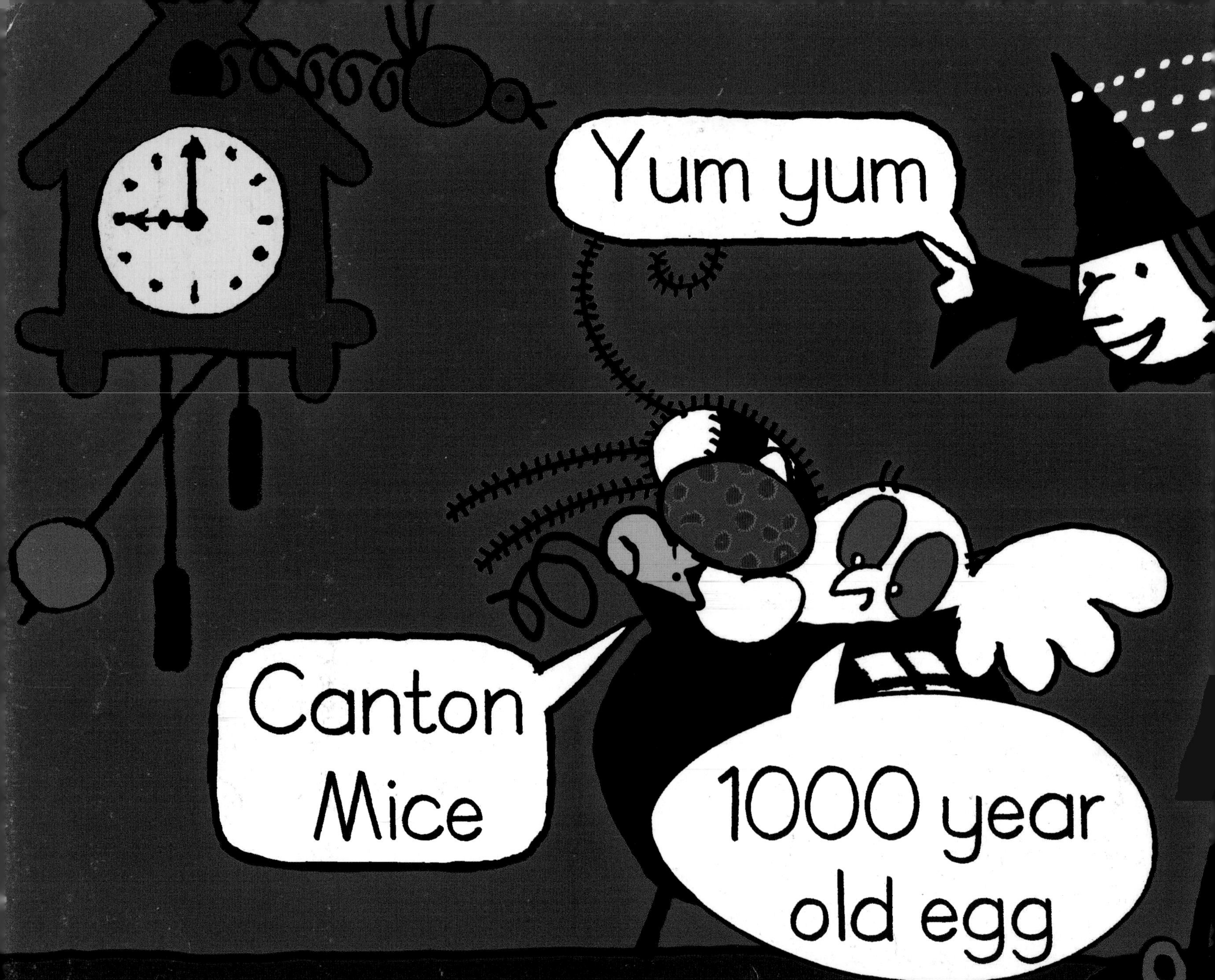

At home they found a treat in the cauldron

They
bobbed
for
apples

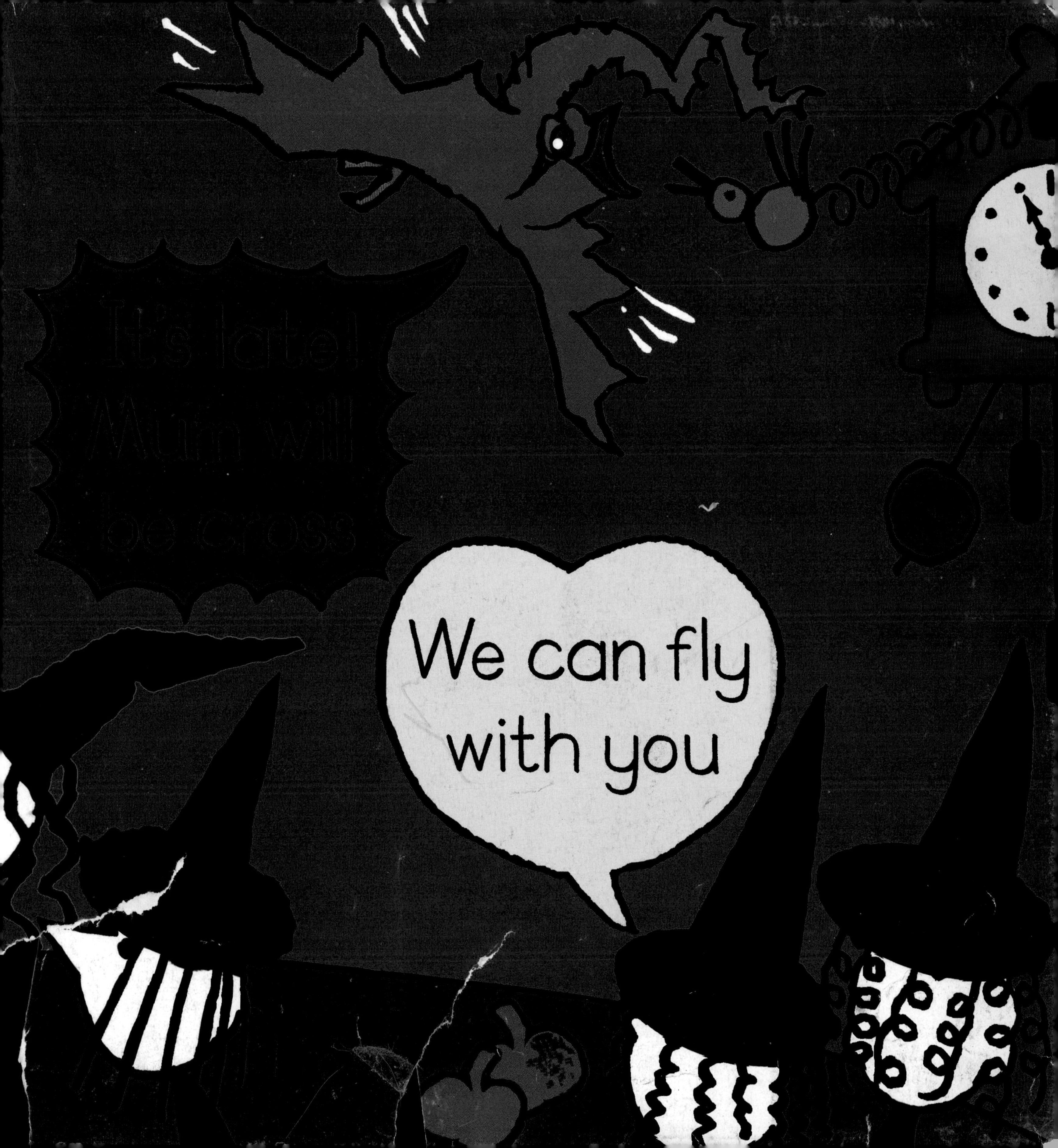
It's late! Mum will be cross
We can fly with you

Goodbye!